The
Chocolate
Lab

TOP DOG

EACH BOOK IS SWEETER THAN THE LAST!

The Chocolate Lab

Tug-of-War

Top Dog

The Chocolate Lab

TOP DOG

By **ERIC LUPER**

Scholastic Inc.

For Ethan
(who keeps me on my toes
more than Cocoa)

Text copyright © 2016 by Eric Luper

All rights reserved. Published by Scholastic Inc., *Publishers since 1920*. SCHOLASTIC and associated logos are trademarks and/or registered trademarks of Scholastic Inc.

The publisher does not have any control over and does not assume any responsibility for author or third-party websites or their content.

ISBN 978-0-545-90243-4

10 9 8 7 6 5 4 3 2 1   16 17 18 19 20

Printed in the U.S.A.   40

First printing 2016

Book design by Sharismar Rodriguez and Mary Claire Cruz

Chapter 1

Triple Trouble

You've got to be nuts if you don't like dog snuggles. There's nothing better than waking up late on a Saturday morning with a warm, fluffy dog sleeping right beside you. I love when that dog lifts its head and then drops it back down, happy to be lying in your comfy bed, too.

Sure, sometimes the dog stretches and pushes you over the edge. Sometimes you wake up to find your face squashed against your dog's rear end. But dog snuggles are the best.

The trouble is that I never get to wake up next to a dog because our Labradors never let me get to sleep in the first place. Our chocolate Lab, Cocoa, has always vibrated with energy. And ever since we adopted Nilla, our yellow Lab, and Licorice, our black Lab, all three dogs have decided they like camping out with me.

That's why I'm so tired while pushing the broom around the old mill my family runs to make our authentic Colonial-era chocolates. The waterwheel turns. The gears clink, clink, clink. And I push my broom slower than a zombie wading in caramel.

"You missed the corners, kiddo," Grandpa says as I bump into his feet.

"Sorry," I grumble.

I know it doesn't sound like it, but the past few months at the mill have been great.

Grandpa Irving makes chocolate the way

we learned to do it from my great-great-great-great-(however many times)-grandmother's cookbook, which we found behind one of the walls of our house.

Dad works in the store. It's been busy, busy, busy with people who can't resist buying our melt-in-your-mouth chocolate.

Mom is the food artist. She takes Grandpa's big bricks of chocolate and turns them into her famous bite-size candies. She grabs a bunch of ingredients you'd never think of putting together and creates something that makes you think you've skipped the dying part and gone straight to heaven.

As for my sister, Hannah, she's too busy to spend much time in the shop since she's gotten involved in animal rescue. She sets up rides for dogs that need to find forever homes. Every Saturday, she meets Ms. Shaw's van to help walk the dogs and give them water. She also brings along a bag of treats for all those excited little guys.

"Try not to kick up so much dust," Grandpa says with a smile. "This store is cloudier than it was behind the artillery line at the Battle of Yorktown." Grandpa is *way* into American history. He even dresses up sometimes and joins in reenactments of the Revolutionary War.

I try to sweep more carefully, but it's tough. The way people made chocolate three hundred years ago is very different from the way we do it now. Although we try to remove the shells from the cocoa beans neatly, they still get everywhere.

I circle back and carefully sweep out the corners, happy that Mom and Dad told me I could start working here. I mostly like it because I can earn some money, but it's fun to hang out in a working chocolate mill anyway. I put in a few hours each day after school and four or five on the weekend.

The bell over the door jingles, and Hannah barges in with Cocoa, Nilla, and Licorice. My sister tosses her backpack on a bench and the dogs start sniffing around.

"When will our dogs understand they're not getting any chocolate?" I say.

"I don't think they ever will. It smells so good!"

I sweep a pile of cocoa shells into my dustpan and dump it into the trash. "Too bad chocolate makes dogs sick," I say. "Could you imagine being around it all the time and not being able to eat a bite?"

Hannah pops a square of plain chocolate into her mouth and smiles. "Nope."

I grab a cloth and start wiping down the

glass pane that visitors look through to see the gears under the mill. Right in the middle, the gear my friend Alan Kunkle and I designed on his 3-D printer smiles at me like a rainbow pinwheel. The mill wouldn't work without it, and it's holding up better than anyone expected.

And none of this would be working without our dogs, that run inside the waterwheel to help get things spinning. They're holding up amazingly well, too!

I move over to the glass case that displays Beatrice Cabot's old cookbook. It sits open to a page where she drew her chocolate-making setup: the heavy chocolate grindstone, her mortar and pestle, and her winnowing basket. A bright red ribbon lies across the page, and I can imagine Great-Great-Great-Great-(however many times)-Grandma Beatrice using it to hold her place in her favorite book.

As I polish the display case, I hear the crunch of gravel in the driveway. A black limousine pulls up.

"I wonder who that could be!" Hannah squeals. "Maybe it's the president! Or better yet, Taylor Swift!"

The driver, a big, burly man in a black hat, gets out. He walks around the car and opens the rear door. A bony man appears. He pushes his floppy brown hair to the side and smooths his jacket.

"Not this jack-a-ninny again," Grandpa mutters.

"Who is it?" I ask, resting on my broom.

His eyes narrow to slits. "The British are coming, Mason. The British are coming."

The man walks along the path that leads to the mill and steps onto the porch.

That's when Cocoa, Nilla, and Licorice pull

free from Hannah's grasp and burst outside. The door swings open and knocks the man back. He tumbles over the railing into a bush. Now all I can see are his legs sticking straight into the air. His pink-and-blue polka-dot socks make me want to laugh.

When he finally crawls out and Grandpa doesn't offer him a hand, I know trouble is brewing.

"**Mr.** Wentworth, I told you no the first time," Grandpa says.

"Call me Charles," the man says. His accent is definitely English. And with a name like Charles Wentworth, I'm surprised he's not wearing a jeweled crown and holding a scepter.

"Okay, *Charles*, Towne Chocolate Shoppe is not for sale."

"But, Mr. Cabot, Regal Candy Corporation is willing to offer—"

"Your offer doesn't matter." Grandpa starts moving the old-fashioned barrels around, something he always does when he's upset. "My name's not even Cabot. That's on the other side of the family. You know nothing about us. You just want to swallow us into your giant company."

The man leans against the counter. "We don't want to swallow you into our giant company," he says. "We want to give you a large sum of money and *then* swallow you into our giant company. You've done a great job here. You're making chocolates for farmer's markets and reenactments. You're starting to find your way into grocery stores. You have the world's only dog-powered waterwheel. If Regal Candy Corporation takes over, we can bring the price of your chocolate down. That will make your brand available across the country—even worldwide. We're talking millions of dollars."

"I told you we're not interested."

Mr. Wentworth smiles. "In time you'll see it differently."

Grandpa smiles back. "No, we won't."

Mr. Wentworth takes a salted caramel chocolate bar from the rack and fishes a few bills from his wallet. "If you change your mind, I'll be staying at the Quarter Inn Hotel," he says. "Good day."

Mr. Wentworth places the money on the counter and returns to his limousine.

"More like *bad* day," Hannah says. "We're not selling the chocolate mill, are we?"

Grandpa kneels in front of Hannah. "We've worked too hard to get where we are. I'm not about to be pushed around by some fancy suit-wearing aristocrat."

"Aristo-what?" I say.

"An aristocrat is a member of high society," Grandpa says. "Like nobility. In Revolutionary times, they'd tootle around in horse-drawn carriages sipping tea. Nowadays, it's stretch limousines and skim soy chai lattes."

I peer out the window as the limousine pulls away. "How much was he offering?"

"The money doesn't matter."

"What if he was offering a million dollars?" I say. "A billion?"

Grandpa hoists a heavy bag of cocoa beans onto his shoulder and starts toward the milling area. "A billion dollars is nothing compared to what we've got."

I look around the mill. Old beams stretch across the ceiling. The waterwheel stands still in the weak stream. "What do we have worth a billion dollars?"

Grandpa turns to me before disappearing downstairs. "We've got plenty."

"Are you hiding a big chest of gold down there behind the grindstone?"

"We've got plenty!" he repeats. "Now get those dogs ready. The waterwheel needs to be turning in a few minutes."

I look to Hannah.

She sits on the floor and gathers Cocoa, Nilla, and Licorice around her. Nilla licks at her face. "I think he means we've got each other," she says.

I sit beside Hannah. Licorice jumps on my lap.

"We'd still have each other if we let Regal Candy Corporation give us a big pile of money," I say.

Hannah strokes Nilla's soft back. Nilla drops onto her side and exposes her belly.

"They wouldn't offer us anything unless one of two things was true," Hannah says.

I let Licorice nip onto my sleeve, and I tug him around the floor. "What's the first?"

"They're scared of us."

"What would they be scared of?"

Hannah shrugs. "That we could hurt their business somehow or threaten them in some way."

"How could we hurt Regal Candy Corporation? They invented the Choco-Whammy and the Caramel Silk Bar. Regal Candy makes practically every candy bar there is."

Hannah scratches Nilla's belly some more. Our tiny yellow Lab's back leg starts kicking. "Yeah, I don't think that's the reason, either."

"Then what's the other possibility?"

Hannah smiles. "Regal Candy knows we're worth way more than a suitcase full of cash."

I smile back and feel a surge of pride. It's

been a lot of work to build our company, get the mill turning, and keep it clean every day. Whatever work I've done, Mom, Dad, and Grandpa have put in ten times that much. The idea that someone wants to pay us money for it feels good. It means we must be doing something right.

A pained whine comes from the other side of the store.

I look at Hannah.

We both leap up and run around the counter. Cocoa is lying on his side, his legs straight out. He has a worried look on his face. He groans. Around him, chewed wrappers lay scattered about.

"Call Mom and Dad!" Hannah screams. "Call 911!"

"What's the matter?" I ask.

"Cocoa's eaten chocolate. Chocolate is poisonous to dogs!"

"**Is** Cocoa going to be okay?" Hannah wails.

Mom hugs Hannah as Dr. Waters, our vet, attaches a tube to Cocoa's foreleg. The tube leads down from a hanging bag that drips clear liquid. Cocoa is lying on a steel table. A bright light beams down on him. His eyes are closed, but his chest is moving up and down slowly.

The last hour was scary. As soon as Hannah screamed, Grandpa charged up the stairs. He grabbed a first-aid kit and squirted some kind of clear liquid down Cocoa's throat. In a few minutes, Cocoa was puking out what he had eaten. Mom raced over with the car, and we brought him straight to the vet.

Dr. Waters checked Cocoa. She looked in his eyes and in his mouth. Then she made him drink some weird-looking black liquid and gave him some medicine that made him fall asleep.

"Is Cocoa going to be okay?" I ask.

Dr. Waters sighs. "He's eaten a good amount of dark chocolate. Even though it tastes as good to them as it does to us, there's a chemical in chocolate that's poisonous to dogs. It's called theobromine, and it's a little like caffeine, the stuff in coffee that keeps people awake."

"We make our chocolate from scratch," Hannah says. "We don't add any chemicals."

"Theobromine is in the cocoa bean from the start," Dr. Waters explains.

"Then why don't they take that chemical out of chocolate?" I say.

"There's really no way to separate it."

Hannah's eyebrows crinkle up, and I can tell she's thinking hard. If there's anything I've learned this past year, it's that Hannah's favorite problems to solve are the tough ones.

Dr. Waters turns to Mom. "We're going to have to watch Cocoa for a few days. We'll keep him here and let you know how things are going."

I place a hand on Cocoa and stick my nose right against his. I can feel his breath pushing in and out. I give him a kiss and try not to look at the drippy tube stuck into his leg.

Hannah pets Cocoa's side. "You'll put him someplace more comfortable, right?"

Dr. Waters smiles. "Of course we will, honey."

"But we didn't bring any of his toys. What if he wakes up and doesn't know where he is?"

Mom pulls Hannah close. "I'll drop some off later this afternoon. Thanks, Dr. Waters."

On the way back to the mill, Mom calls Dad and tells him what's going on. She asks him to gather some of Cocoa's favorite toys and to get over to the mill to reopen. We closed up because Grandpa and Dad had to watch the roasting pans. If you're not careful, the cocoa beans burn, and it ruins the whole batch.

When we pull up to the mill, Dad and Grandpa are just unloading the car. Nilla and Licorice chase each other around the yard. Hannah and I grab the keys and unlock the front door. Then I switch on the lights.

The side window is open. Broken glass covers the floor. The display case is smashed to bits and Great-Great-Great-Great-(however many times)-Grandma Beatrice's cookbook, the one with our secret recipe for Colonial chocolate, is gone!

. . .

After the police leave, Mom and Dad start cleaning up.

"No fingerprints, no witnesses, nothing," Dad says.

Mom starts sweeping. "Who could have done a thing like this?"

"Could've been anyone," Grandpa says, looking closely at the broken display case. "An antique dealer, an art thief, anyone."

Hannah is sitting on the stool behind the front counter. Her feet swing back and forth. "I'll bet it was that British guy in the limousine."

"What British guy?" Dad asks, counting the money in the cash register again. He's already counted it ten times and told the police not a dime was missing.

"He came by earlier today," I say. "He was

from the Regal Candy Corporation. He offered Grandpa all kinds of money to buy the mill."

"Irving!" Mom says. "You can't make decisions like that without talking to us."

Grandpa waves his hand. "The mill isn't for sale."

"Just a few months ago, you told us owning a chocolate shop wasn't a real job," Dad says. "Now you're making business decisions about it?"

Grandpa shuffles around the counter. "This isn't just a chocolate shop. It's a working piece of history. We have a responsibility to make sure it doesn't become a joke. If Regal Candy takes over, they'll cheapen it like they cheapen everything. There will be rides outside, people in mascot costumes jumping around. It will be ridiculous."

"I don't know," I say. "White Chocolate Monkey Bars are pretty good."

"And Marion Monkey is so, so cute!" Hannah adds.

Mom looks at us. "Kids, go outside, please. The grown-ups need to talk."

"When it comes to this chocolate shop, Mason and I are as grown-up as anyone," Hannah says. "Mason invented the plastic gear that helps the grindstone turn, and I was the one who thought of the idea of an overshot waterwheel. If it wasn't for us—"

Mom's stare stops Hannah, and we both go outside. It's just as well, since Nilla and Licorice are still out here playing puppy tag on the lawn.

We sit on a bench and look out at the stream. The sun setting over the trees makes the water look like golden glitter.

"How do you think Cocoa's doing?" Hannah asks.

I can't stop thinking about the drippy tube coming out of his leg. I try to think about his warm dog licks, the smell of his wet fur, and how his snuggles feel when he hops into my bed, but I can't. I'm too sad.

"I'm sure he's doing great," I say.

"I can't stop worrying about him."

"Me neither," I say with a sigh. "We should do something."

"What can we do about a sick dog?"

"Nothing. But we can try to get Great-Great-Great-Great-(however many times)-Grandma Beatrice's cookbook back. Grab your bike. Let's go to the Quarter Inn Hotel."

Chapter 4

Quartered

The Quarter Inn Hotel is a big white building with fancy lamps across the front. Mr. Wentworth's limousine is parked in the lot next door. The driver in the black hat leans against the car reading a newspaper.

"What're we going to do?" Hannah asks.

"I'm not sure yet," I answer.

Just then, Alan rides up on his bicycle. A tiny black helicopter is following him. "Hey, guys."

"What's that thing?" I say.

"It's Herbie, my new drone," Alan says. "I

can control it with my cell phone. So what did you need me for that was so important?"

I tell Alan about Mr. Wentworth and how Regal Candy offered to buy our chocolate mill. I tell him about Cocoa's scary adventure with the dark chocolate. Then I tell him about the break-in.

Alan's eyes get wider with every detail. "We've got to get that book back," he says.

"Exactly."

"Whatever you're planning, it sounds risky," Hannah says.

"Probably," I say.

"Well, I'm not going to be part of this. I'm going home. I have my own plans."

She turns her bike around.

"Don't tell Mom and Dad," I call after her.

"I won't have to," she says as she rides away.

"After you get in trouble, you'll probably beat me home in the police car."

Alan and I turn our attention back to the hotel. "What's the plan?"

"No idea," I say. "Follow me."

We walk over to the limousine. The driver looks over the top of his newspaper at us. He's bigger than Dad, and his nose is crooked.

"Hi," I say.

The driver nods.

"Is this a real limousine?"

"Sure is." His voice is rough, and his words come out slowly.

"Can we look inside?"

He shakes his head.

"We don't get a lot of limos in town," Alan says. "We just want to see what it looks like."

"I can't let you do that," he says.

We sit on the porch of the hotel and look out at our little town. Our mill rests quietly on the water's edge, the waterwheel turning slowly. Across the stream, the front window of our chocolate shop glows alongside all the other small businesses. As the sky darkens, the streetlights start turning on one by one.

I stand up and head inside.

"Where are we going?" Alan asks.

"Regal Candy can't march into our town and push us around. We need to see what's in that limo."

I walk to the front desk. A woman in a red jacket looks at us like we're stinky strays.

"May I help you?" she asks.

"Uh, yes," I say. "Mr. Wentworth is a guest here. He's asked if you could have someone call his driver upstairs to his room."

The woman taps at her keyboard. "What room is Mr. Wentworth in?"

"I think it's 324," Alan says. "But I'm not sure."

The woman taps some more. "I don't see anyone named Wentworth in that room. Oh, wait, I do have a Mr. Wentworth in 227. I'll send someone out right away."

The woman nods to a man standing nearby. His name tag says RUSSELL. Russell heads outside.

Alan and I follow.

By the time we round the corner of the hotel, Russell is already speaking with the driver. In a moment, the two are heading in the side door of the hotel.

"Keep watch," I say. "Warn me if anyone's coming."

"How am I supposed to do that?"

"I don't know. Make a bird sound or

something." I run across the parking lot and slide around to the far side of the car. I know it's wrong, but I open the rear door anyway. The lights inside the limousine turn on. My breath cuts short. Someone is going to see me. I slip into the car and pull the door closed.

The back of the limousine smells like fancy leather, and I sink into the seat. I could get used to riding around like this. Some papers sit on a small table. I flip through them. Most of them are covered in graphs and numbers, but one has words:

Regal Candy Corporation

OLD-TIME CANDY INITIATIVE:

DANDY CANDIES

The purpose of this document is to lay out the plans of the Regal Candy Corporation in its efforts to gain control of the newly created market of old-time candy.

Old-time candy includes licorice, marshmallows, marzipan, pralines, sugarplums, preserved fruit, chocolate, and ice cream.

Companies that produce these products will be acquired and assimilated as soon as possible. Recipes will be brought to Regal Candy Corporation headquarters immediately for analysis and optimization, and the original businesses will be closed down.

Your job, Mr. Wentworth, is to travel around the country gathering these properties for Regal Candy Corporation. Our intent is to open old-time candy shops in

every mall in America. Our stores
will be called Dandy Candies.

I'm not sure what all the words in this letter
mean, but I understand enough to know it's not
good. Grandpa would never be in favor of our
family's secret recipe being used in every mall
in America. He also would not be in favor of
our mill being closed down. I scan around the
back of the limousine, but I don't see anything
else out of the ordinary.

"Ca-caw! Ca-caw!"

Alan is terrible at bird sounds.

"Tweet-a-leety! Tweet-a-leety!"

His screams can mean only one thing.
Someone's coming!

I stuff the letter into my pocket and grab the
door handle. But it's too late. Mr. Wentworth
and his driver are just a few steps away.

Chapter 5

The Chase

"**Mr.** Wentworth, sir," the driver says. "Like I told you already, the hotel people said you called for me. They said you wanted me up in your room."

"Have I ever sent someone to give you a message, Bruno? How do I get in touch with you?"

There's a long pause as I creep over the front seat. "You send a text," he finally says.

"Exactly. I send a text. Was that man a text, Bruno?"

"No, sir. That man was Russell."

"And what might have happened if someone came down here and looked in the car while you were away?"

Another long pause. I press the button to lower the window on the far side of the car.

"They might have found that old book," Bruno says.

"And what would happen if they found that old book?"

This pause is the longest. I climb out the window as silently as I can. Finally, Bruno answers: "Someone would get in trouble."

"Exactly. Someone would get in trouble."

I stay crouched there waiting for my chance to run. It's a good thing it's getting dark out or they would see me for sure.

Suddenly, something buzzes overhead. It's Alan's drone, Herbie. It swoops down at Mr. Wentworth and Bruno. The two duck for cover, and I reach into the limousine and pull the handle to open the trunk. The latch unlocks, and I dive into the nearby bushes.

"What in the world is that thing?" Mr. Wentworth says. "Get in the car!"

Bruno rushes around the limo. His feet stomp right past me, and I hold my breath. He flings open the door, hops in, and revs the engine. Mr. Wentworth gets in the back, and the car pulls out.

I dart into the parking lot, hop on my bike, and pedal after them. Alan follows, one hand on his handlebars, the other holding his cell phone.

"I'm using Herbie to follow the limousine," he calls to me. "Looks like they're stopped at the traffic light near our school."

It's only a block away, but the red light near the school is the longest one in town. It's our only hope. If the limousine gets through, Great-Great-Great-Great-(however many times)-Grandma Beatrice's cookbook might be gone forever.

I pump my legs as hard as I can, pulling away from Alan, who is huffing and puffing behind me. I round the corner by the playground and see the limousine waiting under the glow of the red light. My thighs burn. My hands ache from gripping the handlebars so tightly. But I keep going.

The light at the intersection starts to change, but I pull my bike up behind the limousine and fling open the trunk. Something wrapped in white cloth is sitting inside. It's the shape and size of the cookbook and a bright red ribbon hangs from the folds of the cloth. I grab it, spin my bicycle around, and head toward home.

"Get back here!" I hear Mr. Wentworth yell.

The car turns around and chases us. I'm almost exhausted, but I know this route better than anyone. I've done it every school day since first grade. Down one block, make a right, and head along Maple Lane to the woods. Follow the trail to Main Street, and then it's only a short distance to our house. It's Saturday night, so Mom is probably still working downstairs in the store.

I cut across the corner of Mr. Weinstein's lawn. He hates when kids do that, but right now I don't care. I pedal as hard as I can. After a few seconds, I glance over my shoulder. Nothing. Maybe Bruno and Mr. Wentworth didn't see me make the turn.

I coast for a moment to catch my breath. Suddenly, a pair of headlights swings around the corner, and the limousine speeds after me. I pedal harder than ever. I'm not sure if I'll make it to the safety of the woods, but it's my only chance. Our family has worked too hard to let some big chocolate company take everything away.

My heart pounds. My lungs hurt. The limousine roars closer. It feels as though the car is inches behind me. I don't dare turn to see.

Finally, I shoot into the woods. I cut around a huge oak tree, the one we call home base when we play manhunt. My bike rattles over stones and through ruts where the older kids race their BMX bikes. I splash through a puddle and roll up a hill onto Main Street, not far from where Cocoa found Nilla.

It feels like it's been so long since we were struggling to get the old chocolate mill running, since I became friends with Alan Kunkle, and we figured out how to get that grindstone grinding. But I don't have time to think about any of that now. I just have to get home. I have to run into the chocolate shop and show Mom and Dad that I saved Great-Great-Great-Great-(however many times)-Grandma Beatrice's cookbook, that I saved our business.

I dump my bike on the front lawn, clutch the cloth-wrapped book to my chest, and bound up the porch steps. I fling open the front door and rush inside.

"Mom-you'll-never-believe-what-happened-I-followed-Mr.-Wentworth-to-his-hotel-and-I got-our-cookbook-back!"

Mom is standing there. Her arms are crossed. She wears a stern look on her face.

I hold up the bundle of white cloth. "I got our cookbook back!"

That's when I notice there's someone else standing in the chocolate shop. His arms are crossed, too. It's Mr. Wentworth.

"**What** were you thinking?" Mom says. "You could've been hurt!"

"Mr. Wentworth took our family's chocolate recipes," I say. "He was bringing them back to Regal Candy Corporation so they can open their own old-fashioned candy stores in every mall around the country!"

"Oh, pishposh," Mr. Wentworth says. "I was only here to offer to buy your chocolate mill. Your family told me it's not for sale, and now I'm headed back to deliver the bad news in person."

"But I have the stolen book right here," I say, holding up the bundle of white cloth I swiped from the trunk of the limousine. It's a little muddy from the puddles I rode through, but it's exactly the size of our old cookbook and the red ribbon is still hanging out the bottom.

Mom clears off the counter and takes the bundle from me. She carefully lays it down and unwraps it. It's a blue box that reads BILLY BOB'S FLAT TIRE REPAIR KIT. The red ribbon, or at least what I thought was a red ribbon, is actually a strip of rubber used to patch tires.

"We got a flat on the way into town," Mr. Wentworth says. "Lucky for us it happened in front of Apex Auto Parts. Bruno fixed it in no time."

"But—but—" I try to explain everything I saw and heard, but the words won't come out. I feel my pocket for the letter I took from the back of the limousine.

"Then how do you explain this?" I say, pulling out the folded sheet of paper.

Mr. Wentworth peers at the paper. "How do I explain why you got a sixty percent on your spelling test? I'd imagine it's because you didn't study."

"Oh, Mason," Mom says.

My face gets hot, and I feel the rest of my pockets for the letter from Regal Candy Corporation. It's gone.

"I must have dropped it," I say.

"Mason," Mom says. "I want you to go upstairs and get ready for bed, but first apologize to Mr. Wentworth."

"I'm sorry," I grumble.

Mom shakes her head. "Say it like you mean it."

"I'm sorry, Mr. Wentworth," I say, this time louder but with no more meaning in my heart.

Mr. Wentworth smiles. "I hope we can put this behind us."

I nod, but I know there's no way in the world I'll be able to put this behind us.

• • •

"Are you sure you came this way?" Hannah calls to me through a clump of bushes. "It was dark by the time you got home last night."

"I'm sure," I say, kicking through a pile of dead leaves. "That letter is out here somewhere."

Nilla and Licorice chase each other through the woods around us.

"And you're sure about what it said?" Alan asks. He's wearing a fancy pair of goggles that lets him see through the eyes of his drone. Herbie weaves between the trees, scanning more ground in an instant than we can in an hour.

"I'm positive. The letter said that all old-time candy companies will be bought out and closed down. They want to open these evil stores called Dandy Candies."

Herbie zooms past us to the other side of the trail. The drone glints in the sunlight poking through the high branches. "If they offer you enough money for your business, wouldn't you be happy?"

"Our mill is Grandpa Irving's dream, and the candy shop is Mom and Dad's. The business made those two come together . . . and come true," I say.

"He's kind of right about that," Hannah says. "Even if we had a big pile of money, what would we do with it?"

"You'd roll around in it and throw fistfuls of it into the air!" Alan says. "You'd ride around town in a gold monster truck with a hot tub in the back!"

"How would the water stay in the hot tub if the truck is busy flying through the air crushing cars?" I say.

Alan pulls off his goggles. Herbie gently lowers to the ground next to him. "I just mean you wouldn't have to worry anymore."

"I don't worry," I say.

"Of course you do," Alan says. He folds Herbie's propellers and sticks the drone in his backpack. "Don't you remember when we first moved to town and opened our chocolate shop? Your store almost closed. Then, when you were trying to get that mill running, you had one problem after another. Worry has been a big part of your life."

Suddenly, Licorice tumbles out of the bushes. Something white hangs from his mouth.

"Licorice found a piece of paper!" Hannah says.

We rush over to see. The gold logo for the Regal Candy Corporation—a crown with two crossed swords—smiles up at us.

"The letter!" Alan exclaims.

Suddenly, Nilla bursts from the bushes. She bites onto the other end of the paper and the dogs start playing tug-of-war. Within seconds, the letter is destroyed. My adorable puppies have eaten every scrap.

Chapter 7

No Substitute

Cocoa lies on his side on a soft bed at the vet's office. The drippy tube is still attached to his leg. The bag is almost empty, and I worry what will happen when it runs out. He lifts his head to say hi but quickly lets it drop back down to the pillow.

"Is he going to be okay?" I ask Dr. Waters.

When she smiles, her cheeks glow. "We're giving him every chance he's got. He ate a lot of chocolate, and his body is having a hard time with that."

Hannah buries her face in Mom's sweatshirt.

When Dad wraps his arm around my shoulders, tears rush to my eyes. I fight the urge to cry.

"When will we know anything more?" Dad asks.

"All we can do is wait," Dr. Waters answers. "Feel free to stay awhile. I've got a cat struggling with a hair ball in room two."

"Thanks for all your help, Dr. Waters," Mom says. "We'll stop by tomorrow."

"What about later today?" Hannah says.

"We've got to work at the store. Cocoa will be fine."

But when Mom starts leading us to the car, Dad stays behind to have a few words with Dr. Waters. Just before the door closes, I peek back. Dr. Waters is shaking her head and looking doubtful.

Tears rush back to my eyes, and this time I can't help but cry.

Hannah squeezes my arm. "Mason, do you have some time to help me this afternoon? I have an idea."

I run my sleeve across my cheek and nod. I could use one of Hannah's ideas right about now.

• • •

The farmer's market is filled with people. Tables are piled high with fruits, vegetables, baked goods, and other treats, but Hannah doesn't stop to look at a single thing. She rushes through the crowd like a golden retriever going after his favorite tennis ball. Nilla and Licorice stick by her side.

Finally, Hannah stops in front of McEneny Spice Traders and looks along the rows of jars filled with seeds, teas, grains and herbs. Nilla and Licorice sit at her feet.

She's really done a great job training them.

Mrs. McEneny is sitting on a folding chair. Her feet rest on a crate. She takes a long sip from her water bottle, and a bit of lumpy green liquid trickles down her chin.

"Want to try some?" she offers me.

"What is it?"

"A ginger–kale–whey–green tea smoothie. It's packed with antioxidants and vitamins."

Hannah wrinkles her nose. "It looks like spinach juice."

"It'll make you regular," she says.

I look down at myself. I'm wearing shorts, sneakers, and a T-shirt. "I thought I already was regular."

"No," she says, leaning toward me. "It'll clean out your insides."

I try to figure out what she means by that and decide my insides are clean enough. "No, thank you."

"Do you have any cocoa beans that don't have theobromine?" Hannah asks, peering at the labels on the jars.

Mrs. McEneny puts down her bottle. "Kids usually ask me for candy. Not once in twenty years has anyone asked me for theobromine-free cocoa beans."

"Is there such a thing?" I ask.

"I don't even know what theobromine is," she says. "I can tell you my products are all organic with no additives."

"Theobromine is part of the cocoa bean," Hannah says. "It's natural."

"Then I'm afraid my cocoa beans all have theobromine."

We walk up and down the length of Mrs. McEneny's table. Some lady wearing a rainbow vest and spinning four Hula-Hoops around her waist walks by. She's eating a Venus Bar. Regal

Candy Corporation's gold crown and crossed swords logo sparkles on the wrapper. Hannah scowls at her.

"I do have carob," Mrs. McEneny offers.

"What's that?" I ask.

"It's a bean that tastes similar to chocolate, but it's not. They make carob chips and carob powder out of it. Some people use it for baking."

"Do you have any carob here?" Hannah says.

"I may have a few pounds of it in the truck," Mrs. McEneny says. "Watch my booth while I check."

Before she leaves, she turns back to us. "And don't sneak a taste of my ginger–kale–whey–green tea smoothie while I'm gone."

"You don't have to worry about that," Hannah says.

After she's gone, I poke Hannah. "What are we going to do with fake chocolate?"

"It's not fake chocolate. It's carob."

"It's not better than real chocolate."

"How do you know?"

"If it was, people would have carob shops instead of chocolate shops. They'd sell heart-shaped boxes of carob for Valentine's Day. We'd be making s'mores out of graham crackers, marshmallows, and melty carob!"

"I know that, and you know that, Mason."

"Every person on Earth knows that!"

Hannah smears a sample of natural peanut butter on a cracker and takes a bite. Nilla and Licorice, who I'd almost forgotten were with us, sniff eagerly at the peanut butter, a treat that is totally safe for dogs.

"Every *person* on Earth knows it." She lets Nilla and Licorice lick her fingers. "But does every *dog* on Earth know?"

"Every dog?"

"Just get out your money. We need a pound of carob and a jar of this organic peanut butter. On the way out, we'll have to pick up some chocolate milk, too."

I'm more confused than ever. "What do we need chocolate milk for?"

"I like chocolate milk," Hannah says. "It helps me think."

"**No** way," Mom says. "You can't make dog treats in my chocolate kitchen."

"It's not like there's slimy dog food in them," Hannah says. "It's flour, oats, peanut butter, milk, and carob."

"I still say no," Mom says. "If the Department of Health comes in while you're making doggie treats on my chocolate trays, they'll close us down."

Hannah starts loading all the ingredients into her tote bag. "Fine," she says. "We'll make them upstairs."

I follow Hannah to our apartment. I've been so busy lately that I haven't spent much time here other than sleeping. It actually feels relaxing measuring out the ingredients and mixing them in a bowl for my sister.

I stir the oats, flour, and carob powder while Hannah warms the peanut butter in the microwave and mixes it with some milk. We combine everything until it's a heavy dough, and then we stir in the carob chips.

Hannah starts breaking off lumps of dough and placing them on a cookie sheet. "If Cocoa loves chocolate so much, I thought I'd invent a chocolate treat he *could* eat."

"Maybe it'll settle him down," I suggest.

"What do you mean?" Hannah asks.

"You know how crazy Cocoa gets when he smells chocolate, right? If he can eat something that tastes like chocolate, maybe it won't make him so crazy when he does smell it."

Hannah grabs the cookie tray and slides it into the oven. "Actually, that makes sense. When Cocoa comes home, I'll use these treats to train him better."

A knot twists in my stomach. "Do you think Cocoa *will* come home?"

"Of course I do. Cocoa knows how much we need him."

"That drippy tube makes me nervous."

"It makes all of us nervous," Hannah says. "But Dr. Waters is doing everything she can to make sure Cocoa gets better. She says that drippy tube will help Cocoa. And that kind of makes me feel better."

Hannah always seems to look at the world upside down from how I look at it, but I'm glad she does. Sometimes she makes perfect sense of something that makes no sense to me.

A car pulls up outside. I peek out the window. It's Mr. Wentworth's limousine. He and Bruno get out of the car and walk inside. After a few minutes, they come out, their arms loaded with boxes of chocolates.

I run down to the shop.

"What's going on?" I ask Mom.

"It's amazing!" Mom says, placing a stack of Raspberry Walnut Chunkles into a box. "Mr. Wentworth felt so badly about our misunderstanding that he's decided to buy a whole bunch of chocolate for his family back home."

I glance out the window. Wentworth and Bruno are loading the trunk full with chocolate.

Mom leans close to me. "They bought what we normally sell in a week!"

"Mom, don't you see? They're buying all this chocolate to bring back to their labs. They're going to steal our recipes!"

"Nonsense, Mason. You have to stop being so suspicious. Regal Candy Corporation offered to buy our chocolate shop. We said no. That's the end of it. Mr. Wentworth is just trying to leave on a good note."

Mr. Wentworth comes back inside and hands Mom a credit card. He smiles at me. "Ah, young Mason," he says. "I hope you're not bitter over our little mishap."

I stuff my hands in my pockets. "No, sir."

He takes another box from the counter. "Very good. I'd hate to leave thinking I had an enemy."

"No, sir," I say, this time louder.

"Very good." He turns to leave.

"Mr. Wentworth, are you sure you need this much candy for your family?"

"I have a big family," he says.

I follow him onto the porch. The bell over the door jingles.

"Don't forget your credit card," I tell him, holding it out.

Mr. Wentworth hands the last box to Bruno and takes the credit card. "You're a scrappy little fellow, aren't you?"

I press my lips together so something rude doesn't slip out.

"Well, it's a good thing you didn't look in the briefcase under the front seat of the limousine."

"The briefcase?"

"Great-Great-Great-Great-Grandma Beatrice would have been so proud. It was easy with the side window unlocked. I climbed in, gave the glass case a little love tap with a shiny white rock, grabbed the book, and climbed back out before I could count to ten."

"You can count to ten?"

Mr. Wentworth sneers. His teeth glisten like slick pearls. "Very cute."

I want to run down to the limousine, fling open the door, and look for myself, but I know Mom would be angry.

"Now, have a look at that building over there." Mr. Wentworth points past me across the river.

"The old warehouse?" I ask, looking at the dark building just downstream from our chocolate mill. It has so many broken windows that it reminds me of a rotting jack-o'-lantern.

"I'll bet you barely notice it anymore."

He's right.

"And I'll bet it's so run-down that you can't imagine it returning to use."

He's right again.

Mr. Wentworth kneels down and starts to talk in a low voice. "Well, if you can use that vivid imagination of yours for something other than robbing cars, picture a shiny new chocolate factory there with a beautiful shop in the front that sells all sorts of sweets at half the price of your family's wares."

"You can't do that," I say. "You'd lose money. You'd go out of business."

"Regal Candy Corporation is big. We can suffer losses until your family shuts their doors. We figure it'll take four months at most." Mr. Wentworth narrows his eyes at me. "We offered to buy you out. What other choice do we have?"

"Live and let live?"

"Ah, the innocence of youth," he says. "But who knows, maybe in a few years we can offer you and your sister jobs sweeping up."

Suddenly, the front door of the chocolate shop bursts open. Nilla and Licorice charge out, their tongues hanging from their mouths. They round the mailbox post and brush by Mr. Wentworth, who stumbles backward. He trips over the picket fence and topples into the bush in our yard. His bright purple socks with yellow bananas on them stick in the air.

This time, I do laugh.

Hannah flings open a window of our apartment. A wisp of smoke escapes, and the smell of burning doggie treats drifts down to my nose. Before she has a chance to tell me we need to work on another batch of treats, she sees Mr. Wentworth upside down.

She laughs, too.

Chapter 9

The Shot Heard 'Round the Town

"This is hogwash!" Grandpa barks as we walk across the veterinary clinic's parking lot to check in on Cocoa. Grandpa is wearing his Revolutionary War uniform, probably because he feels like he's going to battle. Hannah and I walk alongside him, but we know better than to say anything when he's this upset.

Mayor Bartley clearly does not know this.

"I'm sorry, Irving," she says, struggling to keep up. "A large company like Regal Candy will bring more than a hundred new jobs to our town."

"It will mean more money in your own pockets. It's exactly what the British did to keep the Colonial leaders loyal."

"Our town is struggling," she says. "We have a chance to change that."

"There are other ways to change things." Grandpa's face is red like the tomato soup he made on the campfire behind our house last week.

"We need the tax dollars," she says. "Our roads are covered with potholes. Our schools need new computers. We're not going to pass this up."

"Mayor Bartley—"

"Irving, this conversation is over. If Regal Candy wants to start making their candy here, we're going to let them. In fact, we're going to make it easy for them."

As she walks away, Grandpa pulls something out of his pocket. It's mostly dull, but parts of it sparkle in the sunlight. "You know what this is?" he asks us.

I look closer. It's a U-shaped piece of metal with what looks like a point sticking out of the middle.

"Is it something old people use to hold up their socks?" Hannah asks.

Grandpa starts laughing.

"It's a spur," I say. "Cowboys use them to get their horses to run faster."

"Cowboys and soldiers," Grandpa says, turning the old piece of metal over in his hands. "This one was used by the American cavalry just after the Revolution. Do you know why I carry it around?"

"In case you meet a horse?" I ask.

Grandpa chuckles again. "It reminds me that even when I don't feel like running, some-times I have to. We've been working hard to make sure our chocolate mill makes the best old-fashioned chocolate in the world. Are we going to let some big company take that all away from us?"

Hannah crosses her arms over her chest. "No way."

I shake my head in agreement.

"Then what do we have to do?" Grandpa asks.

"We have to beat them," I say.

"And how are we going to do that?"

Hannah and I stare at Grandpa Irving as he waits for an answer. All we give him is two shrugs.

"We need to outmaneuver them," he says. "Big companies are like big armies. Ours is like a little group of soldiers. Sure, they're bigger and stronger, but we can move more quickly. If we can find a way to outsmart them, we can take them down. And when a big company like that goes down, they go down hard."

I smile but have no idea what we can do to outsmart a giant company like Regal Candy Corporation. Whatever we do, we'd better figure it out fast. Construction crews started working on the new factory this morning.

I open the doors to Dr. Waters's clinic. The woman behind the front desk brings us straight back to Cocoa.

He looks a little better today. As soon as he sees us, his tail starts thumping on his mattress. Hannah and I rush over and give him hugs and kisses. The drippy tube is still sticking in his leg, but his eyes are bright and he's got a shine in his fur that wasn't there last time I saw him.

Dr. Waters appears in the doorway. "Looks like Cocoa is going to pull through," she says.

"When is the tube coming out of his leg?" I ask.

Dr. Waters steps closer. "That part can be really scary, can't it?" she says. "We'll be taking his drip out once he starts eating on his own. I'd say that will be in a day or so."

I feel a rush of relief. But I won't stop worrying until Cocoa is home with us, curled up in my bed next to me. And even then, I think I'll still have a little bit of worry tucked away inside me someplace.

"Now, you're going to have to promise me one thing," Dr. Waters says.

"Anything," Hannah says.

"You're going to have to promise me that you're going to keep Cocoa, Nilla, Licorice, and any other dogs you know far away from any chocolate."

Hannah and I both promise.

"We actually have a solution for that," Hannah says.

Dr. Waters raises her eyebrows. "You do?"

Hannah pulls one of our newly made doggie treats from her pocket. "It looks like chocolate and it smells like chocolate, but it's not chocolate! We were hoping you might give it your stamp of approval."

Dr. Waters sniffs the treat. "What's in it?"

"Carob," Hannah says proudly. "It's a bean people eat when they can't eat chocolate. It doesn't have any theobromine in it at all, so it should be safe for dogs."

"This . . ." Dr. Waters looks closely at the treat. She sniffs it again and takes a nibble. "Hannah, this is brilliant."

Hannah beams. "Cocoa might not be able to eat real chocolate, but he can eat these all he wants."

"Can you make more?" Dr. Waters asks.

"How many do you want?"

Dr. Waters takes another bite of the dog treat. "How big is your oven?"

Chapter 10

Van of Doom

"**They're** working fast," Alan says as he swoops Herbie the drone down over the Regal Candy Corporation construction site. "They've already rebuilt the roof and the walls."

"It'll be ready in two weeks." I was so focused on Herbie that I hadn't heard Mr. Wentworth sneak up on us. "It's amazing what workers will do when you pay them enough."

"Why are you doing this?" I ask him. "Towne Chocolate Shoppe is no threat to Regal Candy. We're a tiny family-owned business."

"I don't make the orders; I just follow them.

Now, if you'll please fly your drone away from my construction site. I'd hate to have to call Mayor Bartley and tell her you're getting in the way of her plans to make this town great again."

"This town was already great before you got here," Alan says.

"It will be even greater this weekend."

Mr. Wentworth points to a large van at the back of the construction site. The sides are painted red, white, and blue. Right in the middle is Regal Candy's gold crown and two crossed swords.

He pulls what looks like a car remote from his pocket and presses the button. The van chirps, and the side flops down to reveal a small children's carousel with proud, patriotic horses. Carnival music starts playing, and several American flags rise out of the top. They wave back and forth in time with the song "America the Beautiful" blaring out of two large speakers.

"We'll be bringing our van to the farmer's market next Saturday," Mr. Wentworth says. "Free chocolate for everyone."

My face gets hot. "You can't . . ."

"Actually, I can," he says. "I'm not sure you'll be selling much of your chocolate, though. You might want to stay in bed. Sleep late that day."

I can tell Mr. Wentworth sees the worry on my face, so I clench my jaw to hide it.

"Just chasing the good old American dream, kiddo. I'm sure you understand."

Suddenly, Herbie swoops down and almost gives Mr. Wentworth a crew cut. Alan snatches his drone out of the air and stuffs him in his backpack. "Sorry to have bothered you, Mr.

Wentworth," he says. "Mason and I will be sure to stay out of your way from now on."

Puzzled, I follow Alan back to the mill. The waterwheel is turning slowly. The sound of the paddles slapping the water calms me down a little.

"We can't just let him get away with all that," I say. "He's totally cheating."

"In business, there's no such thing as cheating," Alan says. "Okay, maybe stealing your great-great-great-great-(however many times)-grandmother's cookbook was cheating, but this isn't. We're just going to have to figure out a way to outsmart a multi-billion-dollar company."

I think about the messy situation we're in. Everything my family has struggled for seems like it's falling apart. We started off happily making the world's best chocolates until the Kunkles moved to town and opened a fancier store.

Then, after losing the Chocolate Expo, we had to save our shop. Good thing Cocoa was around to discover the secret room behind our wall where we found the old-fashioned chocolate-making equipment. After that, we had problems getting the mill to work: the rush to rebuild, the broken gear, and the weak waterwheel. It's been a stressful roller coaster of a year, and after all that, things are looking worse than ever.

I sit on the edge of the dock and dangle my feet toward the water. Then I hear a familiar snuffling sound behind me. I spin around to see Cocoa limping down the hill. He has a bandage around his leg. Hannah has him at the end of a leash. She's holding a bag that says HANNAH'S CANINE CAROB COOKIES.

I rush over and kneel in front of Cocoa. He licks my face with his warm bologna tongue, and I hug him tight. He still thinks he's a tiny puppy and tries to curl up on my lap. I roll back, and Cocoa lies on top of me. His body weighs heavy on my chest, and I start laughing.

Alan stands over me. "How can you laugh at a time like this?"

"If you can't be happy when your dog comes home, then what's life all about?"

"Well, be quick about being happy. We have a lot of work ahead of us."

I sit up and squint at Alan. "I know exactly what we need to do."

• • •

Later that afternoon, I've called my meeting to order. Everyone is here. Mom, Dad, Grandpa Irving, and Hannah. Cocoa, Nilla, and Licorice. Even Alan and his parents are here with Cotton Candy, their poodle. C.C.'s fur is dyed orange and yellow so she looks like a fuzzy ball of fire.

I wore my fancy button-down shirt so I'll seem more serious. I'm not sure it worked.

Mrs. Kunkle hands a gift bag to Mom. "I almost forgot . . ."

Mom opens the gift bag and pulls out what looks like two shark puppets. She puts one on her hand and opens and closes its mouth. "Uh, thank you," she says.

"They're potholders," Mr. Kunkle says. "My cousin in New York City makes them."

Mrs. Kunkle wipes her hands on her apron. "Normally, we'd bring chocolates, but . . ." She motions to the mill. "I imagine you have enough of that."

"Thank you," Dad says. "Thank you very much."

Hannah takes the shark potholders and starts playing with them, one shark biting the other.

I pace up and down our deck. The stream

glitters behind me. Beyond that, the town rests quietly. "I've called everyone here because we all face the same threat. We're being attacked by the Regal Candy Corporation, and we need to figure out ways to defeat them.

"Oh," Mrs. Kunkle said. "I thought we were coming over for coffee and muffins."

"Muffins?" I say to Alan.

"My parents love muffins," he whispers. "I figured it'd be easier getting them here if I promised them muffins."

"What's this all about?" Mrs. Kunkle says.

"Sorry, Mom. Sorry, Dad," Alan says sheepishly. "But we have an emergency. It's a problem that could hurt us all."

"What sort of problem?" Mr. Kunkle says, concerned.

I point over my shoulder at the construction site. A front loader beeps as it backs across the dirt. Men carry lumber into the building. "Regal Candy Corporation is going to try to put us out of business."

"All businesses try to push out their competition," Mr. Kunkle says.

"Yes, but not like this . . ." I tell them about the flashy van with the flags that plays "America the Beautiful." I explain how Regal Candy Corporation will be offering free candy until we have no choice but to shut our doors. I go on to tell them how Mr. Wentworth admitted in an evil whisper how he smashed the glass case with a shiny white rock and stole our family's secret recipes.

It's that last part that gets everyone's attention.

"How did Wentworth know the rock was shiny and white?" Grandpa says. "Only the police and our family knew that."

"Not even the kids knew . . . He must have . . ." Mom starts.

But Dad finishes her sentence. "Been the one who did it!"

Grandpa's brass buttons sparkle in the sunlight. "We've got to do something!"

Mrs. Kunkle stands. "I'm sorry, but I'm not sure what this has to do with us. We don't make Colonial chocolates."

"Don't you see?" Alan says. "Once Mason and Hannah's store closes, Kunkle Kandies is next! They'll want our factory. They'll want our trucks. They'll want all the contracts we've signed with markets around the country. If we ignore this, we'll be facing the same problems ourselves."

"But if we band together now," Hannah says, tossing carob treats to all four dogs, "we may have a chance to beat them."

Cocoa and C.C. gulp down their treats and bark in agreement. Nilla and Licorice roll around on the dock, tugging on opposite ends of a rope.

"How are we going to fight a huge company like Regal Candy?" Mr. Kunkle says.

They've got many advantages, but we've got one thing they don't . . ." I glance at Grandpa. "We're small."

He smiles.

"We can make quick changes. We can hit them fast and hard and take them down before they even know what's coming."

"The old ambush tactic," Grandpa cries out. "Just like the Patriots did during the British retreat at the Battle of Concord. Sign me up!"

"Does this plan involve muffins?" Mrs. Kunkle says, smiling. "I really do like muffins."

Chapter 11

False Information

Nilla and Licorice sit quietly next to Cocoa, who is curled up on his doggie bed. It's as though they know he's not feeling well and they want to let him rest. Cocoa has been running around some, but I can tell he's still not all better.

Hannah carefully tears along the edge of one of the pieces of parchment paper Mom uses for baking. "The edges have to look rough, but not too rough. And the page has to be just about the same size as Great-Great-Great-Great-(however many times)-Grandma Beatrice's old cookbook."

I move my zombie castle and take Alan's unicorn pawn. We've been playing chess with the set he and I made with his 3-D printer, and I'm getting better. The rules of chess are simple. The tricky part is getting good at it. You have to plan ahead several moves and anything the other person does can change that plan.

Alan glances at Hannah's project. "The page needs to be a little shorter."

Hannah tears off another strip and smiles at her carefully written recipe. "That's about right," she says.

Alan and I both agree.

She crumples the parchment and then smooths it on a cookie sheet. She dribbles Grandpa Irving's leftover coffee on the paper and wipes it with a cloth so the whole page is covered. Then she slides the paper into the warm oven.

"When the edges start to curl, it's finished," Hannah says, tossing out the scraps of parchment on the counter.

"It's not finished until it gets into the hands of the enemy," I say.

"Do you really think Wentworth will take the bait?" Alan says.

"He's already shown us he likes to steal other people's hard work," Hannah says. "There's no reason why he wouldn't steal this, too."

Alan looks doubtful.

We wait a few more minutes. Hannah dumps out Grandpa's old coffee, wipes the counters, feeds the dogs, and takes out two bags of trash while Alan and I focus on our game.

Finally, Hannah returns and pulls the cookie tray out of the oven. Alan and I gather around to see her handiwork.

Lying there before us on the warm tray is an old-looking recipe—an old-looking *fake* recipe.

"Now to set our trap," Hannah says.

• • •

"I'm telling you," Hannah insists as we walk past the Regal Candy construction site. "Our new, super-secret recipe for old-fashioned *spiced* chocolate is the best we've ever made."

Out of the corner of my eye, I see Mr. Wentworth watching. He's pretending to look at his cell phone, but there's no mistaking it. He's paying close attention to us.

"But Regal Candy Corporation already has all our recipes," I say.

"They don't have *this* recipe," Hannah says, taking the parchment from her pocket. "This one was in the safe. It's the one that

Great-Great-Great-Great-(however many times)-Grandma Beatrice made for George Washington and his troops at the Battle of Saratoga. This chocolate will be better than anything Regal Candy Corporation can ever make."

"I don't know," I say. "Regal Candy is giving their chocolate away for free."

"But this recipe is famous! People will pay for famous!"

We sit on the curb, our backs to the construction site. It takes all my willpower not to look at Mr. Wentworth. He moves behind the oak tree near the sidewalk.

"Mom and I made a sample batch last night." Hannah takes a bar of plain chocolate from her backpack and hands me a square just like we planned. I pop it in my mouth and try my best not to overact.

"Oh, this is the best!" I exclaim. "It's no wonder George Washington was able to win the Revolution with chocolate this good. It's sure to sell a million bars!"

"A billion," Hannah says as she looks at her watch. "We better get home. Mom, Dad, and Grandpa Irving are going to need help with this recipe."

Hannah and I get up and head to the mill. We don't turn to see if Mr. Wentworth notices what we left behind. We run up the stairs to the loft where Alan is sitting on a large bag of cocoa beans. His fancy drone goggles cover his eyes.

"Wentworth is moving closer," Alan says. "He's looking up and down the street."

"Make sure Herbie stays out of sight," I say.

"He's flying high. No chance he'll see me."

"Herbie's loud," Hannah says.

"He's quiet from so far away." Alan takes off his goggles. "And Wentworth took the bait."

"Good," I say. "I was afraid he'd see right through our story."

"Why's that?" Hannah asks.

"George Washington wasn't *at* the Battle of Saratoga. It was General Horatio Gates. Don't you listen to Grandpa?"

Hannah wrinkles her nose. "Not when I can help it. Now, let's get ready for the farmer's market. We've got a lot to do."

Chapter 12

This Means War!

After talking about it for a few days, Mom, Dad, and the Kunkles agreed they should combine their two companies. The Kunkles are better at making deals with stores while Mom and Dad are better at making chocolate. The Kunkles also have the machines to make more chocolate and the trucks to get it out into the world.

After arguing over whether the new company should be called Kunkle Cabot Chocolates or Cabot Kunkle Chocolates, I suggested Patriot

Chocolates. Everyone loved it, and we had red, white, and blue labels printed up right away.

For the rest of the week, Hannah works her tail off on her carob dog treats.

Mom, Dad, and Grandpa Irving work their tails off on making chocolates.

Mr. and Mrs. Kunkle work their tails off on new deals with supermarket chains and one with a large mall a few towns away.

Alan works his tail off on his drone-flying skills.

As for me, I work my tail off on making fresh lemonade. I know it sounds silly, but it's all part of the plan.

Hannah, Alan, and I get to the farmer's market extra early so we can set up. Hannah has been working with all three dogs in her free time, and they sit quietly while we work. Mr. Wentworth and Bruno are already there wearing Uncle Sam suits and tall top hats. Bruno's suit stretches tight across his belly, and his hat looks tiny on his giant head.

"We'll be handing out free chocolate all day," Mr. Wentworth says to us. "You may want to bring out your folding chairs. You'll be sitting down a lot today. "

"Actually, I think it's going to be busy for us," Alan says. He pulls Herbie from his backpack and taps at his cell phone. Herbie's propellers buzz.

I uncover a wagon loaded with three coolers of fresh lemonade and stacks of paper cups. I've got three more coolers stowed under the table. Hannah unrolls a sign advertising her carob dog biscuits. When she starts lining up the jars of treats, Bruno laughs.

"She's selling doggie bones!" he says.

"I see you're finding new little businesses

for yourselves," Mr. Wentworth says. "Good choice."

"Oh, this is just a little side project I'm working on," Hannah says. "Dogs deserve the taste of chocolate, too."

"And people love lemonade," I add.

Mr. Wentworth straightens his hat. "You probably should have sold us the company when you had the chance."

"Maybe you're right." I put a water bowl on the ground for the dogs. Licorice drinks some. Cocoa and Nilla follow. Nilla stumbles. Her muddy paws land in the water. "But in business, sometimes the most unexpected things can happen."

Mr. Wentworth walks across to us. "In business, nothing is unexpected. When I push the button on our truck and that carousel starts spinning, the people of this town will rush over here like trained monkeys. They'll eat our chocolate, fall in love with it, and forget all about you and your family. In a few months, Regal Candy Corporation will buy your chocolate mill cheap. You watch what these trained monkeys will do."

Alan unfolds his laptop, plugs in his cell phone, and starts tapping away.

Before long, a crowd starts to gather at the farmer's market. Almost everyone in town shows up, maybe more than came to the grand opening of our mill. Reporters from local television stations park their vans nearby and start talking into microphones. A few even have the nerve to ask us what we think. Hannah, Alan, and I make sure to only say nice things, but I can't resist sneaking in the line I'd planned: "I think it's great," I say. "Competition only makes the world spicier!"

Finally, Mr. Wentworth stands on a platform and raises his hands. The crowd quiets. The cameras point at him.

Alan puts on his goggles, turns on Herbie, and sends him up into the air to record the entire event.

"Ladies and gentlemen . . ." Mr. Wentworth's voice blares through speakers mounted on the top of his brightly painted van. "Thank you for coming to the world premiere of Regal Candy Corporation's newest craze . . . old-time chocolate!" He pushes a button on his remote. Confetti cannons pop red, white, and blue streamers into the air. The crowd cheers.

"We know you've tried other Colonial chocolates, but experts tell us our recipe is the one George Washington fed to his troops at the Battle of Saratoga!"

Some people clap, others look confused.

"Each bar has been wrapped with a copy of the original handwritten recipe, which we have uncovered through years of hard work!"

Hannah laughs. All three of our dogs—black, yellow, and brown—sit at attention, watching Mr. Wentworth.

He holds his remote over his head. "Is everyone ready to taste history?"

The crowd cheers again.

Wentworth presses the button. The side of the van opens. Patriotic tunes blare from the speakers. Confetti cannons fire again. The carousel starts turning. Mr. Wentworth and Bruno start tossing chocolate bars to the crowd.

People snatch them from the air. They tear off the wrappers and stuff the chocolate into their mouths.

"So what's the secret ingredient you added?" Alan asks.

"Chili powder," Hannah says. "Lots and lots of chili powder."

It doesn't take long for the cheers to turn to moans. People start to gag and spit out their chocolate. Some start wiping at their tongues to get the spicy taste out of their mouths.

News reporters can barely speak, but the cameras keep filming. Alan steers Herbie above us, his own camera aimed at the mayhem.

Within seconds, people flock to our table to buy lemonade. They toss money at us, grabbing cup after cup. Before long, our pockets are stuffed with cash, and everything we had to drink is gone.

"Everyone! Please settle down!" Mr. Wentworth says. "What about George Washington? What about the Battle of Saratoga?"

"George Washington wasn't even at the

Battle of Saratoga!" Mayor Bartley calls out, taking another swig of her lemonade.

"This chocolate is perfectly fine," Mr. Wentworth says. "I'll eat some myself to show you!"

"Boss," Bruno warns. "It's really spicy. You might not want to—"

"Nonsense." Mr. Wentworth rips off the wrapper and takes a huge bite of Regal Candy Corporation's newest chocolate bar.

His face turns pink. His eyes start tearing. The chocolate bar drops from his hands.

"Wawa . . . Wawa . . . Wawa!!!" Wentworth starts running around the van looking for something to drink. He rushes over to our booth waving his hands at his mouth. "Wawa! Wawa!! Wawa!!!"

Hannah and I shrug.

"We're all sold out," I tell him. "I guess our little business is doing okay."

Mr. Wentworth looks around for anything to cool off his tongue. He dives to the ground and picks up the dog bowl. It still has a little muddy water sloshing around at the bottom.

He lifts the bowl to his lips and drinks it all down.

"And that's the end of Regal Candy's new product line," Hannah says.

Chapter 13

Carob Empire

By the time Mom, Dad, and Grandpa see the news reports, the farmer's market has settled down. The news vans have disappeared. People have either gone home or are shopping for fresh veggies. And Mr. Wentworth and Bruno are packing up their van.

"What happened down here?" Mom asks.

Mr. Wentworth stomps over. "I'll tell you what happened. Your awful children have ruined our event. We spent thousands of dollars setting this up, and you're going to pay back every penny of it!"

Mom puffs up like a big grizzly bear. "First of all, no one calls my children awful. Second, you've done nothing these past few weeks but . . ."

As Mom digs her claws into Mr. Wentworth, Dad and Grandpa walk over to us. "Don't mind your mother," Dad says. "She's under a lot of stress."

"Mr. Wentworth deserves it," Hannah says.

Grandpa laughs. "Not many people deserve it more."

"We'll be right back," Dad says. "We need to talk to Mrs. McEneny about getting more cocoa beans. Thanks to the Kunkles, Bistro Supermarkets wants to try our chocolate in all their locations."

"That's got to be fifty stores," I say.

"More like two hundred and fifty!" Grandpa boasts, and they walk off.

I turn to Hannah. "How are we doing on the carob dog treats?"

"Not great. There's been so much distraction with the spicy chocolate that no one's really come over to try them."

"Well, *our* dogs like them."

Cocoa, Nilla, and Licorice sit at Hannah's feet staring at the glass jars. Nilla's tongue darts out and licks her nose. Licorice jumps up and puts his front paws on the table. It's a stretch for him, but he reaches.

"Shoo, you little pests," Hannah says, giggling.

The dogs run off and start playing in the grass.

"How are we doing on the video?" I ask Alan.

"Almost finished," he says, tapping furiously at his laptop. "I got audio of Wentworth. Herbie got video of people spitting out their chocolate right in front of the Regal Candy van. I'm just setting it to music and throwing in some graphics . . ." He taps a little more on his laptop. "And it's posted!"

"Where did you post it?" Hannah asks.

"YouTube. A few other places." Alan squints at the screen. "Whoa, it already has a dozen views."

Just then, Dr. Waters walks over. "I told Ms. Shaw from the dog transport to meet you here rather than the usual spot."

"Oh, I totally forgot!" Hannah says. "I hope she's not upset."

"Not at all. She understands. And I have some great news."

I hear barking in the distance. It gets louder. Suddenly, a dozen or more puppies come charging down the grassy hill behind us. Ms.

Shaw is chasing them, her Fur-ever After Rescue and Transport fleece tied around her waist.

The dogs slam into our table and knock it and the jars of carob dog biscuits to the ground. Nilla and Licorice run over and all the dogs—ours and the rescue animals—start eating the treats.

"I guess this means your dog biscuits are tasty," Dr. Waters says.

"You would know," I say. "You ate one yourself."

"What I think and what dogs think are two very different things."

Hannah and I stand the table back up and put the empty jars in the wagon. "So what's the good news?" Hannah asks.

Dr. Waters places her hand on Hannah's shoulder. "I hope you don't mind, but I gave a few of your treats to my friend who works for

Purity Dog Food. He said they've been looking for a product just like this, and they're ready to offer you bundles of money for your recipe."

Hannah doesn't smile. She doesn't jump up and down. She just stands there watching the dogs gobbling up her carob doggie treats.

"Cool!" I say.

"Not cool," Hannah says, crossing her arms.

Dr. Waters frowns. "What's not cool about it?"

"I'll only do it if money from each bag goes to support animal rescue."

Dr. Waters levels her eyes at Hannah. "I knew you'd say that, and they've already agreed."

Hannah bursts into a smile and hugs Dr. Waters.

"If it all works out, we're going to build a brand-new shelter for the town! Ms. Shaw will have a place to bring as many puppies as she can save, and we'll be finding more homes for dogs than ever!"

A tear sneaks out of the corner of Hannah's eye, and she hugs Dr. Waters even harder.

"Your children have stolen from me!" Mr. Wentworth hollers at Mom. "They've attacked my customers. Your dogs have knocked me into bushes not once but twice! And I think my neck is starting to hurt! You'll be hearing from my lawyer as well as the lawyers from Regal Candy Corporation!"

"They'll be hearing from no lawyers," Mayor Bartley booms. She storms over with her phone in her hand. "I've seen the video about how you're trying to put these good people out of business, how you think we're all trained monkeys!"

"I never said that!" Mr. Wentworth chirps.

Mayor Bartley holds up her cell phone. The screen starts flashing Alan's video. Mr. Wentworth's voice sounds loud and clear.

"When I push the button on our truck and that carousel starts spinning, the people of this town will rush over here like trained monkeys.

"Trained monkeys!!

"Trained monkeys!!!"

Alan edited the video to zoom in on Mr. Wentworth's face every time he repeats himself. You can see his pearly teeth glisten as he snarls into the camera.

"This changes nothing!" Mr. Wentworth roars. "Regal Candy Corporation will make our own old-fashioned chocolates. We'll march across this country jamming our delicious treats in the mouths of every man, woman, and child!"

He flings open the van door to get in. Something falls out.

Bruno lumbers over to pick it up, but a brown blur streaks across the ground and gets there faster.

Cocoa!

He snatches up whatever fell and brings it back to me as though it were a Frisbee I'd just tossed.

"It's Great-Great-Great-Great-(however many times)-Grandma Beatrice's cookbook!" I say.

Mom turns on Mr. Wentworth, but he knows better than to stick around. He jumps in the van and drives away—red, white, and blue confetti swirling in the breeze behind him. Bruno looks down the road, then back at us.

He starts running after the Regal Candy Corporation van into the distance.

Cocoa sits down and places the cookbook at my feet. I pick it up.

"He got dog drool all over the pages," I say to Grandpa. "He bit holes in the cover. It's ruined."

"It's not ruined," he says, wiping the book with his sleeve. "We're just a part of its history now."

I flip through the pages. "What if Wentworth stole all the recipes? What if he copied the whole book or took pictures of everything with his phone?"

"It's not about the recipes, Mason. None of this is." Grandpa kneels down and looks me straight in the eyes. "What's important are the minds behind it all. You and Hannah have made us proud these past few months. We know that no matter what the world has to throw at us, our team will get through it."

I look at Mom and Dad, at Hannah and Alan. And I know what Grandpa said is true. A billion dollars is nothing compared to what we've got. Things have been strange this past year, for sure, but we've tackled everything that's come our way as a family.

Suddenly, puppies swarm around me from all sides. I sit down on the grass and let them jump on me. Nilla, Licorice, all of Ms. Shaw's rescue dogs, and on top of them all, Cocoa pushes through with a big, fat, slobbery, love-filled lick.

Not everyone loves the feel of a dog's tongue on your cheek or the smell of its fur or the warmth of a snuggle. But I do. And when Cocoa's the dog in question, there's just nothing sweeter.

Did you miss the first sweet story?

Read on for a sneak peak at how Cocoa's
delicious adventures began!

Chapter 1

Doggy Disaster

There are two kinds of people in this world, the kind who like dog licks and the kind who don't. I'm that first kind. I like the feel of sloppy, smooth dog tongue on my hand. I like warm dog breath in my face. I like knowing each drop of slippery slobber means my dog loves me no matter what. Most days my mom and dad are dog-lick people, too.

But not today. Today my parents want nothing to do with Cocoa's tongue or any of the rest of him. Today they just want a do-over so they can keep Cocoa out of the chocolate laboratory at the back of our chocolate shop and away from the display my mother was working on for next week's big Chocolate Expo.

"That dog . . ." my mom says as she looks at what's left of her workshop. "That . . . dog . . ."

Those are the only two words she says, but I can tell the rest of them are bunched up inside her mouth and want to burst right out.

I try to change the subject. "Did you ever think how amazing it is that we have a *chocolate* Labrador retriever with a *chocolate* name who lives in a *chocolate* shop who goes completely bonkers when he smells *chocolate*? It's like a miracle right here in our own house!"

And it's true. Cocoa may not be allowed to eat chocolate, but he can sniff it out from a mile away. When he does, he gets more excited than a cat with a noseful of catnip. I guess Cocoa is like me that way, because when I get an idea I can't sit still until I do something about it, too. Maybe that's why I know what he did is not actually his fault.

"I just wish our little miracle pooch would stay out of the workshop," Dad says. "How many times have we told you to put Cocoa in his crate when Mom is working?"

"I did," I say. "I remember locking it and everything."

"If you had locked Cocoa's crate, he wouldn't have been able to do this," Dad says. He dumps a tray of chocolates into the garbage. The smushed, smashed, totally mangled candies slide into the can with a *thumpity, thump, thump* louder than Fourth of July fireworks. Call me crazy, but I think they still look yummy.

"This isn't the first time, Mason," Mom says. "You're going into fifth grade. What have we told you about responsibility?"

I'm not sure if this is one of those don't-answer-it-or-you'll-be-in-big-fat-trouble questions, so I'm glad when my little sister, Hannah, walks in from our apartment upstairs. Her eyes roam over the mess. Pots and pans of every size litter the floor. Trays are upturned. Dark, gooey chocolate splatter covers everything like spin art gone wrong. Chocolate is even dripping from the ceiling!

Hannah narrows her eyes and looks around some more. "*Humph*" is all she says.

Mom puts her hand on Dad's arm. "Bill, even if I work twenty-four hours a day for the next week, there's no way we'll be ready for the expo. Not to mention the cost of what that dog . . . That . . . dog . . ."

Miss Meredith, Towne Chocolate Shoppe's only employee and definitely not a dog-lick person, begins straightening boxes next to the cash register. Cocoa waddles up next to me and noses at my hand. I know it's not the time for petting, but I give him a quick one anyway. He licks my fingertips.

"What if we all pitch in?" I say. I pick up a large spoon and straighten it as best I can. It's still bent.

"I couldn't do it with an army of Oompa Loompas," Mom says. "If Mel Kunkle could see us now, he'd be laughing his head off."

Mel Kunkle. Just the name gets my dad's face redder than a bowlful of cherry filling. Three years ago the Kunkles moved here from the big city with what Dad calls "big-city money." They also came with big-city ideas of how to put our small-town chocolate shop out of business. Not only did they put ads for Kunkle Kandies on every billboard, park bench, and diner place mat in town but they also bought a giant machine that burps out more chocolates in an hour than we can make in a week. People line up just to get a peek at the machine in their front window.

"No one is interested in quality anymore," Mom says, placing a drippy pan on the counter. "They want fancy gizmos and bright blinking lights. When Grandpa Irving gets here, we'll ask him to stay the week like we discussed."

"The week?!" Hannah and I say at once. Grandpa Irving is my dad's father, the side of the family that knows nothing about the magic of candy making. His idea of a fun weekend is dressing up in old army clothes, sleeping in a leaky tent, and pretending he doesn't know what electricity is. He never stops talking about the American Revolution, which is probably because he's old enough to owe George Washington a quarter.

Dad makes uggy-buggy eyes at Mom and she nods. It's how they talk to each other without words.

"We were going to take you guys for pizza to talk about this, but you might as well know now," Dad says. "We need to start thinking about the future. College for you two. Retirement someday. Even though we love Towne Chocolate Shoppe, we can't go on struggling. Your mother and I are going up to Glens Falls to see about a few things."

Mom drops a spatula and some dipping forks into the sink. "We may have to move in with Grandpa for a while, just until we sort things out."

"How long is a while?" Hannah asks. "School starts soon. I'm going to be head pirate in the fall musical. Mrs. Pratt said so when I saw her at the supermarket."

Dad unplugs the chocolate warmer. "One of

the reasons we need to go to Glens Falls is to look into school for you guys," he says.

"But what about the store?" I say.

Dad sighs. "Business has dropped off since Kunkle Kandies came to town. We were hoping the Chocolate Expo would help us get back on our feet."

"We can only keep this place open if it's making money," Mom adds.

"What about Cocoa?" I say. "Grandpa's building doesn't allow pets."

Mom slides the registration folder for the Chocolate Expo into the trash and cups my face in her hands. "Try not to worry, Mason. Your father and I will figure something out."

I look past Mom to the garbage can, and it looks like they've already figured out plenty. If that folder had a tongue, it would've been sticking it out at me.

Cocoa makes a chuffing sound as though he wants me to pull the folder out. Then I realize he's trying to tell me his superpowerful ears hear someone coming up the walk.

The door swings open and Miss Meredith stuffs her cell phone into her pocket. "Welcome to Towne Chocolate Shoppe," she says brightly. When she sees who it is, her smile vanishes and she pulls out her cell phone again.

Grandpa Irving is standing there with a suitcase tucked under one arm, a bundle of rolled-up maps under the other, and a tattered tricorn hat on his head. His eyebrows look bushier than ever.

"Where are my two favorite grandkids?" he bellows in his big-belly voice.

"We're your only grandkids!" Hannah says like she does every time he says that.

Grandpa looks around the store. "Sheesh,

did Virginia's Second Regiment march through here or something?"

Dad explains what happened while I go over and give Grandpa the strongest bear hug I can.

He fake groans from my squeeze and bends down (this time giving a real old guy achy-back groan). Maps spill from under his arm. "Don't you worry about this," he says. "Everything is going to be just fine."

But everything isn't going to be just fine. Towne Chocolate Shoppe, our family business, is going to close. Hannah and I will have to go to a new school, away from all our friends. And worst of all, Cocoa is going to live in some kennel somewhere with a bunch of dogs he doesn't even know.

I look for Hannah so we can figure out what to do, but she's already stomped away.

MEET RANGER

A time-traveling golden retriever with search-and-rescue training . . . and a nose for danger!

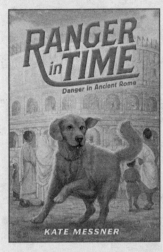

THE PUPPY PLACE

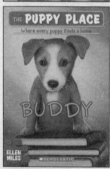

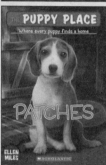

WHERE EVERY PUPPY FINDS A HOME

Puppy Powers